No Place Like Home

A STORY ABOUT AN ALL-BLACK, ALL-AMERICAN TOWN

Hannibal B. Johnson

EAKIN PRESS ✤ Fort Worth, Texas
www.EakinPress.com

Published By Eakin Press
An Imprint of Wild Horse Media Group
P.O. Box 331779
Fort Worth, Texas 76163
1-817-344-7036
www.EakinPress.com
1 2 3 4 5 6 7 8 9
ISBN-10: 1-68179-138-2
ISBN-13: 978-1-68179-138-8

Contents

Acknowledgments

Special thanks to Donna Berryhill, Cheryl Brown, Cindy Driver, André Good, Tré Good, Henrietta Hicks, Arlene Johnson, Kimberly Johnson, Jodie Larsen Nida, and Joshua Ravenell. These individuals graciously consented to review drafts of this work. They offered important feedback and insights.

Author's Note

This story, set in 1920, revolves around Charles "Charlie" Jackson, a twelve-and-a-half-year-old from Boley, Oklahoma, one of America's best-known all-black towns. Today, Boley, once a thriving black mecca, is smaller and more subdued. Still, significant historical footprints line her streets and alleys.

Charlie's window on the world offers us an up-close and personal view of this historic town during its heyday. In an era of great flux—the immediate wake of World War I; the dawn of women's suffrage; the rapid industrialization of America; the introduction of the doomed social experiment known as Prohibition; the continuation of unstable race relations and racial hostility, intimidation, and violence against African-Americans—Boley became a kind of cocoon enshrouding African-Americans ("coloreds" or "Negroes" at the time). They thrived, emboldened

vii

and empowered by the sense of openness and opportunity the town provided.

Through Charlie's eyes, we re-visit the importance of self-esteem, of believing in oneself and one's unlimited potential. Through Charlie's eyes, we re-examine what it means to be part of a family, to have deep roots. Through Charlie's eyes, we re-discover some of the values that help create a sense of community: love, faith, charity, hope, perseverance, and integrity, just to name a few.

Charlie's experiences illuminate a little-known slice of American history. In the process, they highlight important lessons for our present lives and for our futures.

Introduction

There's no place like home. "Home," that simple, yet powerful, four-letter word, means different things to different people.

Home is a house—a physical space, a place of shelter from the elements, a place of rest and repose. Home is an address.

Home is family—a group of loved ones, together under a single roof, not just physically, but emotionally as well. Home is a hearth.

Home is community—a physical and an emotional space defined by shared rights and responsibilities, not limited by blood kinship, and open to all who are open to it. Home is a village.

Charlie inhabits all of these homes. Deep inside, he harbors a profound calmness. He feels both connected and protected. He feels like he belongs. He finds, as you may have likewise found, that there's no place like home.

CHAPTER 1

A Place Called Home

Learn as if you were going to live forever.
Live as if you were going to die tomorrow.

—MAHATMA GANDHI

For Charlie, home is a little town called Boley (pronounced "Bow-lee") nestled right in the middle of Oklahoma (well, almost in the middle), equidistant from Oklahoma City and Tulsa. You might say it's "in the boonies" or "in the sticks" since it's a small town out in the country.

Boley sits along the Fort Smith and Western Railroad. Like a lifeline, the railroad connects Boley to other towns, promoting business and commerce.

In Boley, there are churches, schools, banks, grocery stores, hotels, restaurants, department stores, a telephone company, an electric company, an ice plant, a movie house, and more. The town has everything you'd find in any other small town. Main Street brims with activity every day: busy people coming and going, others just milling about the thoroughfare.

A Boley native, Charlie has always been proud of his heritage and his roots. He loves telling his story in his own words and in his own way.

"I was born and raised here. My folks moved to Boley in January of 1905, just a few years before I was born.

"I'm twelve-and-one-half years old. I'll turn thirteen in about six months, on January 27, 1921. I'm tall for my age, five feet, eleven inches and growing. I weigh one hundred and fifty-one pounds. I wear size nine-and-one-half shoes. My parents say that if I keep sprouting like a beanstalk, I'll have to sleep with my legs dangling over the edge of a too-small bed. I know I'll have my Dad to thank for it if that happens. I get my height from him.

"I have brown eyes, curly black hair, and mahogany-colored skin. Oh, yeah, I've got a big, broad smile. Mom says it lights up the room!

"I'm as big as a lot of grown-ups, but I figure I still have a lot of growing up to do. I guess brains don't grow as fast as bodies.

"I'm an only child—no brothers or sisters. I know, I know! That's supposed to make me a spoiled and selfish kid. Honestly, though, I don't think that I'm the least bit spoiled or even a tad selfish. I don't get everything I want, and I certainly don't always get my way.

"My parents taught me to be considerate of others—to try to understand their circumstances and appreciate their feelings. My folks also made sure that I had other kids to play with when I was younger so that I wouldn't be lonely and I'd learn to share and to take turns. I never felt like an only child and I certainly never acted the part! So, whoever said that the only child in a family always turns out to be a spoiled, selfish brat got it wrong—at least this once!

"I've lived in the same slate blue, two-bedroom 'shotgun' house at the end of a *cul-de-sac*, 1863 Spruce Street to be precise, my whole life. By the way, in Boley, streets running north and south are named after trees, like my street, Spruce; streets running east and west are named after former presidents of the United States, like Lincoln and Grant.

"In case you don't know, a shotgun house is a long, thin, wooden house shaped like a giant rectangle. It's called a shotgun house because people say you could shoot a shotgun right through the front door of the house and the bullet would travel in a straight line all the way through the back door. Since the house is laid out like a long, narrow shoebox, the bullet would pass through almost every room in the house. It might even wind up in the outhouse.

"Where are my manners? Speaking of things you don't know, I should introduce myself. My name is Charles Jackson. Most of the kids at school call me 'Charlie.' But my close friends, my best buddies, my real pals, call me 'PK.' That's short for 'preacher's kid.'

"My Dad, Hezekiah Jackson, is the minister at Antioch Baptist Church. Folks call him 'Reverend Zeke.' Dad's tall and lean—six feet, four inches, one-hundred ninety pounds, to be exact. He's athletic looking. His voice is deep and kind of gravelly. It's the kind of voice other preachers envy. If Dad's size doesn't get your attention, then his voice definitely will!

"My Dad's probably a lot like most dads. He may be a little stricter, though. I have chores—mowing the lawn, washing the dinner dishes, and cleaning my room, for example. I have an 8:00 P.M. curfew on weekdays and a 10:00 P.M. curfew on weekends. I have some responsibilities at my church—helping maintain the grounds, assisting with the offering during services, and a couple of other little things. I'm required to do my homework every night, and to get good grades.

"For doing all those things, I get an allowance. I deserve it, and boy, does it come in handy!

"I know that you must think my Dad is pretty tough from what I've told you. Sometimes, though, things with hard shells are really soft on the inside. That's my Dad! Once you get to know him, he's as soft as a marshmallow roasting on an open fire!

"To know my Dad—to *really* know him—you've got to know something about our church. That's his heart and soul—his passion!

"Antioch Baptist Church is a small, red-brick building surrounded by a dense clump of sycamore trees. The church opened in 1905. It's nothing fancy, but it's spotless, inside and out. Dad wouldn't have it any other way. 'Son, this is the Lord's house, and we must respect that,' he often reminds me. 'That means dressing up, being on your best behavior, and keeping things neat and clean.'

"Antioch Baptist Church is not just my Dad's church. My Grandma and Grandpa belong to the same church, too. I guess you could say it's the Jackson family church.

"If you're looking for me on a Sunday, you'll likely find me in church, right around the middle pew on the right-hand aisle. Chances are I'm wearing my Sunday best: a charcoal gray suit, a crisp white shirt, a black bowtie, and black lace-up shoes. If services are in session, I'm sitting straight up, back flush against the hard, wooden seat, eyes fixed on the pulpit, arms at my side, hands folded in my lap. You know how soldiers stand at attention, right? Well, you might say I'm *sitting* at attention, if that's possible.

"I'm thinking, 'respect, respect, respect,' and I'm watching out of the corners of my eyes to see who's watching me. When you're a PK, some-one's almost always watching, especially in church. I know that if I do something wrong, I'll have to answer for it, if not to Mom and Dad, then to some other adult.

"If I'm not actually in church on a Sunday, it's likely that I'm on the way or I've just left. Most PKs don't have much choice in the matter. Dad says that Sunday is the Lord's Day, and that the least we can do is give the Lord one *full* day out of seven.

"Being the only son of a well-known pastor isn't always easy. Sometimes the other kids tease me. They call me names like 'preacher man,' 'the right reverend,' and 'holy roller.' It's tough some days, but hey—'sticks and stones,' right?

"Occasionally, other kids make fun of the way I talk, too. They say I sometimes 'talk funny' and sound 'too proper.'

"My parents insist that I speak properly, using only correct grammar—'good English,' as they say. My Mom even talks about things like 'diction' and 'elocution.' That's just the way I've been brought up. I'm not doing it because I think that I'm better than anyone else.

"My folks say that a person who speaks well will almost always be more successful than one who doesn't. I believe that. Besides, I know how to use slang as well as the next kid. I just know when to use it and when not to.

"It isn't just the kids that can be a problem for me and my fellow PKs. Sometimes adults expect too much from me, maybe because of my Dad's position in the community. He's a leader, so they assume that everything about him, including his family, must be 'just so.' They all seem to think that everyone in the family should be perfect, and never make mistakes.

"Nobody's perfect. I'm certainly not even close, but I do my best, especially in school.

"This year, I'm taking mathematics, language arts, life sciences, physical education, and music. Right now, I've got all As! That's not because I'm perfect; it's because I study hard!

"Even though I set high standards for myself, I still make my fair share of mistakes. In fact, I can be as naughty as the next kid sometimes—I'm no goody-two-shoes, that's for sure! I'm still learning. Isn't that what being a kid is all about?

"Speaking of learning lessons, I once did something with a buddy that really taught me a thing or two. I hopped a freight train with my pal, Stephen. We thought it'd be fun to sneak on the train, ride a mile or so, and then hop off without being caught. We got caught.

"I got in trouble, but not as much as I thought I might. Mom sat me down and we had a long talk. She got all emotional, saying she didn't want me to end up like some vagabond, looking for free rides, moving from place to place, and calling no particular place home."

The conversation Charlie had with his mom lasted only a minute or two, but it made a lasting impression on him. It stuck with Charlie because it came at an important time in his life—a time when he'd just begun to experiment and to assert his independence.

"Son, baby, you don't want to wind up like some hobo or tramp or bum, now do you?" Charlie's mom pleaded, her petite frame bending ever so slightly toward Charlie.

"Now, you know what those folks are, don't

you, baby? A hobo is a worker who moves from place to place, catching a free ride on a train when he can. A tramp is somebody who just moves from place to place, on a train if he can find one, not caring at all about finding work. A bum is somebody who doesn't go anywhere and doesn't do anything.

"Hobo, tramp, or bum," Charlie's mom continued, "it's a dangerous, scary life that you don't want to lead, Son. You don't want to be any one of the three, so you'd best get yourself straight! You don't usually get something for nothing, Son. If you do, it won't last," she sighed, her straight, coal-black hair hiding sad almond eyes.

With that, Charlie's mom slipped out of the room, leaving him alone to mull things over. Then and there, he vowed to himself that he'd never hop another train. He'd learned his lesson, once and for all! He reflected on what had just happened.

"I'm sure you've done something you're not supposed to do, right? All kids do! There's a little bit of what my Mom calls 'roguishness' in all of us! Whether it's hopping a freight train, sneaking an after-bedtime snack, staying out past curfew, playing hooky from school, or some other 'no-no,' we've all done things that are against the rules. Of course, getting caught is no fun. Getting punished is even worse. I just try not to make the same mistake twice.

"I'm not special. I'm a regular kid with regular likes and dislikes; with regular hopes and dreams. I wish that people could understand that.

"I like people—almost all people. Getting to know people is fun to me—the more, the better! I think that I can get along with anyone who'll give me a chance.

"I like fun and games. Hide-and-go-seek, billiards, darts, checkers, chess—you name it, I like it. I also collect Lionel trains. I order some of them from the Lionel catalogue. Sometimes, I get them as gifts. I'll bet being a train conductor in real life makes for a swell job!

"I like life. I'm just like you—no better, no worse. I'm what you might call an 'average joe,' except for the name, of course. I guess people could call me the "average Charlie," but that would sound pretty funny, huh?

"Even though I may look a little older, I like the same things most kids my age like. I like curling up somewhere—almost anywhere—with a good book. I prefer fast-paced, exciting books like *The Return of Sherlock Holmes*, *Stories from the Arabian Nights*, and *The Adventures of Tom Sawyer*, but sometimes I'll go for an interesting biography. I'm amazed at how some people manage to rise from almost nothing and become successful, sometimes even famous.

"One of my favorite biographies is about Abraham Lincoln. Now there's a brave, courageous and honorable man—a true American hero. Imagine serving as president when he did—

during the deadly Civil War between the North and the South. Just think about what he did for our country: ending slavery and holding the Union—you know, all the states—together.

"I also enjoy reading about the lives of other great men like Frederick Douglass, the famous abolitionist, and Booker T. Washington, the world-renowned educator. Lincoln, Douglass, and Washington combined smarts and courage to do great things for the world. When I grow up, I want to do something for our country that will make me as famous as they were.

"Although I love books, I'm not a total book-worm. My nose isn't always in a book. I'm what Dad calls 'well-rounded.' That just means that I enjoy doing lots of different kinds of things.

"I like playing baseball with the neighbor-hood kids out in the field behind my house. I pre-fer to pitch, but I'll play any position. I like being part of a team, depending on others, and having them depend on me. When everybody works hard and works together, my team usually wins.

"Speaking of baseball, I want to go to a Negro League game the next time some teams go on a barnstorming tour. You know, don't you, that colored players aren't allowed in big league base-ball? So, they play in the Negro League, which is made up of teams with all-colored rosters. They tour the country playing exhibition games. That's called 'barnstorming.' Hey, who knows—maybe someday everybody will be able to play together in one league!

"Dad says that one of these days he's going to take me to a big league baseball game. Just think, I might even get to see last year's World Series champs, the Cincinnati Reds. They just whipped the Chicago White Sox five games to three.

"Never mind that the White Sox threw the Series. Some of the White Sox players took bribe money and agreed to make sure that the Reds won the game. I think that the Reds would have won without that help, but we'll never know now. That whole 'Black Sox Scandal,' as folks are calling it, put a stain on baseball that's going to be hard to remove. I still love the game, though. It'll take more than a few crooked players to ruin the game for me!

"Well, that's enough about baseball. I like lots of other things, too.

"I like riding the giant, multicolored Ferris wheel at our yearly town carnival. I get goose bumps from being way up in the air looking down on all the people. They look like tiny ants on a mission. They seem to scurry about in every possible direction, running from the reds and blues and greens and yellows and oranges flashing down on them from the spinning sky wheel. As neat as it is, though, riding the Ferris wheel is not my favorite thing to do.

"Guess what I like more than anything else? Most of all, I love going fishing with Dad. When it's just the two of us, there's something special."

CHAPTER 2

One More Thing

We have flown the air like birds and swum the sea like fishes, but have yet to learn the simple act of walking the earth like brothers [and sisters].

—DR. MARTIN LUTHER KING, JR.

Y ou already know some things about Charlie. You know where he lives. You know how old he is. You know what he looks like. You know what he likes to do. But there's one thing about Charlie that you don't know. Charlie is "colored." Some people say "Negro" instead of colored, but they mean the same thing.

Just about everyone else in Charlie's hometown is colored, too—even the big shots! In fact, a local fellow who goes by the name "Uncle Jesse" put it this way:

> *Oh, 'tis a pretty country*
> *And the Negroes own it too,*
> *With not a single white man here,*
> *To tell us what to do—in Boley.*

The police chief and the fire chief, the doctors and the lawyers, the teachers and the preachers—they are all colored. The businesses—Farmers & Merchants Bank, the Boley Electric Company, and the Boley Telephone Company, to name a few—are all colored-owned. The Boley Town Council is all-colored, too. That's what makes Charlie's little town different from some others, and probably different from yours.

Charlie isn't really sure how important that label, "colored," is for him. After all, aren't we all *some* color?

"My Dad says that being colored is not just about skin color, although some folks will tell you that. It's really about something called culture. When I asked him what that meant, he said, 'Son, when people are together for a long time, they develop strong bonds. They come to share many common characteristics and practices. They may share a common language, physical traits, diets, and more. They begin to like and dislike many of the same things. They may face common problems, and work together to solve them. That's culture.'

"So, I guess Dad just meant that culture is like a larger version of family. And I guess I'm part of the colored culture, huh? I'm not sure I understand all this culture stuff, or even why it matters. Maybe I will someday. Maybe you already do.

"Believe it or not, I used to wonder whether

the whole world was made up of colored people like me. It's not quite as silly as you might think. Back when I was just a little kid—only six or seven years old—I only knew what I'd seen. I'd never even seen the rest of the state of Oklahoma then. In fact, I'd never traveled outside my hometown of Boley—except in my dreams, that is.

"Most of the people I saw looked a lot like me. Of course I knew that not everyone had my big chocolate-brown eyes, or my round, freckled, button nose, or my short, wavy black hair. But one big thing that we all had in common was that we were all considered colored people, despite our physical differences.

"Our skins ranged in shade from mahogany brown to coal black to the color of coffee with too much cream. Inside that word 'colored' there sure seemed to be a lot of, well, color!

"Our eyes, though often brown, may be blue or green or any number of other colors. Our hair went from thick and coarse to thin and fine. Some of us can—and, according to my Dad, some of us do—pass for white.

"Now that I'm older, I realize that there are all sorts of people in the world, not just colored ones. Most people are pretty much the same when you really get to know them.

"One of my friends is white. His name is Stephen, and he's the boy I hopped the train with. He's the only boy in one of the few white families in our town. Well, I say Stephen's my friend, but sometimes it doesn't seem like it. Friends do everything together, right? Well, we don't. Actually, we don't even see one another that much. We do play together sometimes on weekends, but we attend different schools and churches. That's the way it is around here with our laws and customs. Because of segregation, there are many things that colored people and white people can't do together.

"It's too bad that Stephen and I can't be closer friends. We're so much alike it's unbelievable. We both love books and sports and movies—oh, and trains, too! We definitely could be best friends if things were different around here. I guess we're just unlucky. We're different in the one way that makes being best friends almost impossible.

"I'm colored, that's for sure. But everybody's really colored in some way—shades of black, white, red, brown, and yellow. It's just that not all people are 'colored' like me. People come in all colors, shapes, and sizes, but we're all people. Mom and Dad say that I should treat them all with respect.

"I'm working on memorizing a poem about respect. It's one of my folks' favorites, and it's called 'The Iceberg.' No one seems to know who wrote it, but Mom and Dad think it's very special. Here's how it goes:

The Iceberg

I'm like a giant iceberg,
I'm more than what you see;
Really get to know me,
Imagine what might be.

Don't think that I'm not human,
No, I'm really just like you;
But I'm also like an iceberg,
'Til you know me through and through.

My eyes, my nose, my lips, my hair,
See them as I do;
They are not the answer,
They won't tell you who.

I may not talk like you do,
I may speak a different way;
But listen for the meaning,
In all of what I say.

My clothes may be tattered,
Not the latest style;
But it's the inside not the outside,
That matters all the while.

I may be red or yellow,
I may be black or white;
Look beyond my color,
Whether dark or light.

I may be rich, I may be poor,
I may not fit right in;
It's not about the money,
It's the person who's within.

Really get to know me,
My beauty you will see;
Get to know the real me,
That's the only way to be.

You may think you know me,
You might even fence me in;
But before you put me in that box,
Find out where I've been.

I may be who you think I am,
I may be more or less;
But you won't know, you never will,
Until you see my best.

You may think I'm funny,
You may even fear;
But don't be quick to judge me,
Just draw me ever near.

Though we may be different,
In a way or two;
We share much in common,
In what we see and do.

Treat me like I'm family,
Show me some respect;
We'll get along much better,
Each other we'll protect.

When we come together,
Out of many one;
To focus on our future,
Our journey yet begun.

Together we have power,
Divided we have none;
Let's decide, let's take a stand,
You and me as one.

I'm like a giant iceberg,
I'm more than what you see;
Really get to know me,
Imagine what might be.

"I wish the world could really be that way; that people would recognize that what we look like on the outside is not who we are on the inside. But I know that color matters; that people like me—colored people—are not always treated with respect.

"Dad always reminds me that even despite the problems we face, we are a blessed people. One thing's for sure: I'm proud of who I am.

"I get my pride from my parents, especially from my Dad. He's always telling me about family achievements and about other people with what he calls 'can do' attitudes. That makes me feel like I can do anything I set my mind to do. Dad tells me that all I need to do is set some personal goals, believe in myself, and work hard. Dad's shorthand for that is 'conceive, believe, and achieve.' That's what I try to do."

CHAPTER 3

The Perfect Day

*The best and most beautiful things in the
world cannot be seen or even touched.
They must be felt with the heart.*

—HELEN KELLER

Each day is a gift. Life in a small town in rural America like Boley offers a cornucopia of simple, natural pleasures. Occasionally, the gift, nature, and people come into near-perfect alignment. Charlie had one of those days.

"Just last Saturday, we went on a daylong fishing trip. Our day began at about six o'clock that morning, but my adventure started hours earlier. When I get excited about something that's coming up, I dream about it the night before. I can't imagine anything much more exciting than a fishing trip, can you?

"Drifting off to sleep Friday night—it was 10:30, I believe—I remember thinking, 'I can't wait until tomorrow!' In the fog of my dream, I imagined an ideal fishing trip with Dad at an amazingly beautiful, crystal blue lake. The fish seemed particularly friendly, almost anxious to be caught. We simply threw in our lines and Zap!—they attracted the fish like magnets: big ones. We caught so many fish that we released half of them. We only kept what we knew we'd be able to eat. Everything that day seemed perfect, too perfect to be real. My dream ended as fast as it had begun."

The next morning, the bright orange summer sun inched up on the horizon and beamed through the half-open white curtains hanging in Charlie's bedroom window. The sun's warmth and glow—and the chatter of the mockingbirds in the backyard—awoke him from his Saturday slumber. He jumped out of bed as if he'd been stuck with a needle. He hurriedly washed up in the basin in his room. Then, he threw on a pair of wrinkled, denim overalls and a pair of well-worn work boots before racing to meet his father in the kitchen.

There at the counter Reverend Zeke stood, a towering presence, sipping piping hot, jet-black coffee from a well-worn ceramic mug and scanning the week's *Boley Progress*, the local newspaper. The nutty coffee aroma lit up the room like a full yellow moon brightens up a pitch-black night sky.

Reverend Zeke believes that coffee is not for kids, so Charlie's never actually tried it. One of these days, though, Charlie's bound to sneak a sip and see whether the smell matches the taste. The sense of mystery surrounding this adult beverage, combined with Charlie's natural mischievousness, makes it inevitable.

At the kitchen counter, Charlie and his dad packed their sack lunches. Reverend Zeke nimbly drew the kitchen curtains to allow the toasty, bright rays of the sun to illuminate their workspace. They stuffed their crumpled, brown paper bags with dark purple grapes, sweet red apples, figs from the backyard tree, sandwiches made of smoked ham and cheddar cheese on dark rye bread lightly glazed with mustard, and homemade oatmeal cookies with raisins. Charlie longed for the traditional fare his mom routinely prepared.

"As much as I love sandwiches, they're nothing like Mom's meals. A ham sandwich just doesn't compare to her home-cooked delights. It's like a Thanksgiving feast around here most days.

"Just thinking about Mom's cooking makes my mouth water with anticipation for a typical family feast: juicy, golden-brown fried chicken; freshly picked black-eyed peas; mixed collard and mustard greens seasoned with meaty ham-hock and wild onions; pan-fried, hot-buttered cornbread; and flaky-crusted sweet potato pie for dessert. Now that's a *real* meal!

"Well, I know that there will be plenty of home-cooked meals to come, so today I'll have to make do with the food we've got. Oops! I almost forgot about our drinks."

Charlie pulled a sixteen-ounce Mason jar out of the creaky kitchen cabinet, filled it with water drawn from the well out back, and carefully closed the lid.

"Don't forget about me, Son," Reverend Zeke urged, his tone both respectful and commanding.

Charlie reached into the cabinet a second time, repeating the steps he'd just taken. Now armed with two jars of thirst-quenching well water and two mouth-watering sack lunches, the pair was almost ready to go.

Once they'd prepared their food and water, they grabbed their bait, a large jar of plump, squiggly, pink earthworms and a rusty, dented pail filled with swirling, silver minnows. Then, Charlie slipped two slender bamboo fishing poles out of the back of the shed. The thin, white string on the fragile poles tangled them together as he eased them from their resting place. Charlie gently separated the poles while his father neatly wrapped each pole's string.

Just as they were about to head out, Charlie's mom called him into her bedroom.

"Here, honey," she said. "Take this quilt with you to sit on."

Charlie insisted that they didn't need a quilt, but his mom refused to budge. So, he took the homemade, hand-woven bedcover from her arms.

"Look at the color and the pattern, Son," Charlie's mom suggested, pointing proudly to her handiwork. "Those bright colors make it easy to see from a distance. That was important to our African ancestors because of tribal warfare and because they were hunters who needed to keep an eye on one another.

"The diamond pattern represents the cycle of life," Charlie's mom noted, her index finger gently outlining one of the several diamond patterns sewn into the quilt. "Each of the four points of the diamond stands for one of the parts of the life cycle: birth, life, death, and rebirth. So, honey, you're holding something very special. Take good care of it."

Charlie's mom, whom folks called 'Sister Corrine,' smiled faintly, but proudly. She turned toward Charlie, extended her arms, and pulled him close. She gave him a big hug and a quick peck on the right cheek.

"Alright, Mom, I will," Charlie pledged, as he eased away from her embrace.

After saying goodbye to his mom, Charlie and his dad hopped in the family's new black Ford Model T, fresh off the Detroit assembly line. Charlie's pocket watch read precisely 7:20 A.M.

They headed for their favorite fishing hole, a little pond behind the Dukes' rock house located just a short drive away. Although the pond was located on private property, the Dukes generally did not object to its use by members of the community. Of course Reverend Zeke and his boy, being upstanding church folk, were always welcomed with open arms by the Dukes.

Mr. Dukes, a quiet, fair-skinned man with straight hair, is a kind soul. He does road maintenance work. Although his wife is a steadfast Baptist, he's Methodist. They make an interesting couple indeed.

Mrs. Dukes is a persnickety woman. She's confident, yet careful, with a kind of subdued sophistication. At about five-feet, six inches tall with pecan-toned skin, she has a pleasingly plump build that gives her a handsome, stately silhouette. Her clear and precise diction matches her meticulous personal presentation: hair coiffed in a severe bun; flawless make-up; black dress; stylish hat; black heels; matching black purse; gloves, typically white; and, of course, hose. That's the Mrs. Dukes most folks know.

After a rather bumpy ride on a gravel-and-rock-covered dirt road, Charlie and his dad arrived at their destination: the Dukes' pond. They found a convenient spot to park the car, and then hiked over to their usual spot on a small, light-green, grassy hill along the banks of the pond. They draped Sister Corrine's quilt of many colors over a bed of soft grass shaded beneath the canopy of a weeping willow tree. Charlie and his dad unloaded their supplies and gear, and then positioned themselves comfortably on the quilt. They baited their hooks, sacrificing the worms first and saving the unsuspecting minnows for later in the day.

It seemed as if they were winding up and getting ready to hurl the first pitch of the World Series. They cocked back their poles and flung their lines into the cloudy, gently flowing water. The hooks hit the water with a quick thud. Two small splashes erupted. Then, the water stood strangely still. As if expecting a strike, they eased back, relaxed, and waited for the fish to bite. They waited and waited and waited.

"Dad," Charlie asked impatiently, "How long do you think it will take before we catch something?"

"Son," Charlie's dad replied in a slow, lilting tone, "If you want to be a great fisherman, you've got to learn how to wait. Fishing is a lot like life. Both require hefty portions of patience and determination, and neither comes with a guarantee."

"Well," Charlie responded, "I guess you're right. We've got all day, and we won't ever catch anything if we don't give it a try."

As usual, the waiting gave Charlie and his dad a chance to talk things over, to really get to know one another. They talked and laughed while they watched and waited. They talked about everything—church, school, sports, girls, food, politics, books, music, and more.

Charlie even confessed that he'd gone skinny dipping in Mrs. Dukes' pond once. "All the kids do it," he argued in his own defense.

Reverend Zeke grinned broadly at the revelation, knowing full well that he, too, in an act of boyish defiance, once skinny dipped in a similar pond. For a brief moment, he'd been transported back in time to his own boyhood. He, through Charlie, remained forever young.

Despite the revelation, Charlie did more listening than talking. Most of all, Charlie loved to hear his dad talk about music—all kinds of music. His dad always seemed eager to oblige. This time, Charlie's dad enlightened him on the origins of the blues.

"Workers back in the slavery days created what's called 'field hollers,' to while away the time. Most of our folk worked in the fields, planting and poking and picking. Like spirituals—church songs—field hollers were 'call and response,'" Reverend Zeke continued, almost as though delivering a sermon.

"An elder or other respected person among the field hands would lead the workers in the holler. They weren't sung, they were yelled; they were hollered. That's how they got their name. The workers responded to their leader's 'call' with a 'response.' That's why it's called 'call and response.'

"Then," Reverend Zeke continued, "the tempo of the holler and the pace of the work moved according what task the workers had to perform. In a way, fields became stages for the workers' magical, field holler-driven rhythmic dance.

"I recollect a cotton-picking field holler that the old folks used to chant when I was young. It went something like this, Son:

"Bend down low, bend down.
Chop that cotton, chop 'round.
Startin' up in the early mornin'.
Workin' right up 'til the evening sun.
Gonna pick up all that cotton.
Gonna make sure none's forgotten.
Work on, work on, work on.
All King Cotton gonna be gone."

"Wow, Dad," Charlie nodded, "I never knew that those old songs had so much meaning. I just thought of it as a bunch of moaning and groaning by some old folks. I'll see things differently from now on," said Charlie apologetically, his gaze cast downward.

"You know, Charlie, I'll bet you could come up with your own field holler if you really tried," his dad suggested, coaxing Charlie with a gentle challenge.

"Just think about one of the chores you do around the house. Now I know there's some down home misery that you could holler about. C'mon, now, it'll do you some good to let it all out."

"Dad," Charlie said haltingly, "You might just be onto something. You know how I dread mowing the grass. Let me think for a minute."

After a forty-second pause that seemed like an eternity, Charlie finally mustered the courage to give it a try. "I think I've got it, Dad," Charlie volunteered.

"Pushin' that mower goin' 'round and 'round.
Cuttin' that grass, down, down, down."

"Go, Son, go!" Charlie's dad exclaimed. So, after another short pause, Charlie finished the holler—he "took it home," as his Dad would later say.

"Sun's blazin' and the sweat does pour.
Just a boy doin' a man's unhappy chore.
I do what I'm told, I do what I must.
No harm workin', in that I trust.
Pushin' that mower goin' 'round and 'round.
Cuttin' that grass, down, down, down."

"Whoa, I did it!" Charlie exclaimed. "I actually made my very own field holler, Dad! I'm a composer, huh?"

"Yeah, Son, I suppose you are a composer now," Charlie's dad chuckled. "I reckon we've all got a little composer deep down inside us!"

"Enough about field hollers, Son," Reverend Zeke exclaimed. "Let's talk about something we both love: the blues."

"Oh, yes," Charlie retorted, "The blues—my favorite type of music! Boy, how I love the blues!"

"The blues, Son, come directly from those field hollers we just talked about," Charlie's dad noted. "The two are as related as a chicken and its egg."

"Really, Dad?" Charlie intoned.

"Yes, really, Son," his dad replied. "Those

field hollers turned into songs. Folks sang the songs *a cappella*, meaning without musical instruments, at first. It'd be pretty hard to carry 'round instruments, let alone play them, while you're working in a cotton field, huh, Son?" Reverend Zeke asked, not expecting an answer, but just making a point.

"Some folks say that we call these songs 'blues' because they're usually about people who are blue—you know, down and out, suffering and sad. Others say they're called blues because of the special way the tones come together—the sound of the chords and such. One thing's for certain: We all know the blues when we hear them!

"At first, no one bothered to write these songs down. In fact, folks just made them up as they went along—that's called 'improvising.'

"Nowadays, we have fancy composers, musicians, and singers, and a lot of music is written down. We've even got some music celebrities these days. Why, it's amazing how popular that fellow W.C. Handy is today! He's getting such a reputation that folks here have taken to calling him 'The Father of the Blues.' His tunes like *Memphis Blues, St. Louis Blues, Joe Turner Blues,* and *Beale Street Blues* are all the rage!

"With all the juke joints and speakeasies springing up since Prohibition, and with the war just ended, it's a fine time to be in the blues business. There's some real money to be made, and I'm not talking about nickels and dimes!"

Charlie loved these conversations. He wanted to know what his dad thought about the things that mattered most to him. He also felt confident that his dad wanted to find out what was in his head, too. Charlie figured this time was his chance to talk and to listen, one-on-one, and he always made the most of it.

The minutes and the hours just slipped away. Before long, it was time to go home. And guess what? Though they'd caught up with one another's lives, they hadn't caught up with any fish.

Initially, Charlie thought that the trip had been a disaster—nothing like his dream. After all, he wondered, how can a fishing adventure be successful if you don't catch any fish?

Usually they catch something—a big perch, a fat crappie, or a long-whiskered catfish. This time, though, neither of them got even the slightest nibble. The only fish they saw that day were the minnows they'd brought for bait. Minnows don't make much of a meal—at least not for humans.

Though they didn't catch anything, at least nature cooperated, giving them a calm, clear day. One thing they saw plenty of was the sun. Though they took advantage of the shade as best they could, the scorching heat of the Oklahoma summer could not be escaped. The gentle, dusty Boley breeze helped, but it couldn't stop the sizzling summer sun from sapping their energy.

Weary and just a bit disappointed, they

headed home around 2:00 in the afternoon. As they rounded the corner onto Spruce Street, they could see Sister Corrine on the open porch in the distance. There she sat, framed by the color burst of blooming flowers in her well-manicured flowerbed, shelling string beans in the steamy summer heat.

Charlie and his dad exited the car and approached the porch. Sister Corrine, perched there in her wooden rocker, took a big gulp from her large glass of sweet tea.

Looking up ever so slowly, she remarked, "So, boys, where's dinner? You know I was counting on frying up a great big fish feast for us this evening."

Heads hung low, Charlie and his dad stuttered and stammered something that translated into, "We struck out."

"Well, boys," Sister Corrine continued, chuckling under her breath, "I guess we'll have to move along to Plan B, then. I reckon I'll be frying up some yard bird this evening. Bless your hearts.

"You know, boys," Sister Corrine continued, "I used to fish with Daddy—Grandpa Joe—when I was a little girl. Believe me, we caught some mighty fine fish back in those days. Fact is, we fished in the same pond you just visited. Daddy took me along more often than not. I know most girls didn't get to do that. They spent their time quilting, canning, picking, planting, and doing all manner of household chores—'women's work,' they called it. Well, Daddy didn't believe in 'women's work.' He'd say time and time again that work is work. He'd say to me, 'Princess, ain't nothing you can't do if you work at it. Nothing.' Before long, I began to believe him.

"Anyway, boys, fishing always reminds me of Daddy and how he worked on my spirit. He made me the strong woman I am today. You see, it wasn't the fishing that mattered so much as spending time together.

"Now, you fellas may not have caught anything on this particular trip, but you did spend some quality time together. Count your blessings!"

With that, Sister Corrine retreated to the kitchen, leaving the menfolk on the porch. As usual, she created a feast worthy of kings. Fish or fowl, Charlie's mom managed never to disappoint.

Sister Corrine was right, as usual. Despite their bad luck, Charlie's spirit soared. He was so happy that he'd spent the whole day with his dad. As odd as it may sound, Charlie's Saturday fishing adventure in Boley made for the perfect day. Catching a few fish would have been nice, that's for sure. Just being out there in the company of his dad, though, proved to be more than enough for Charlie.

Think about it: If you could do anything you wanted on your own special day, what would you do? Would you prefer an outdoor adventure like fishing or camping? Would the latest Hollywood movie catch your fancy—something featuring a big star like Charlie Chaplin or Mary Pickford or Douglas Fairbanks; maybe a film like *The Homesteader* by that colored producer/director, Oscar Micheaux? Maybe you'd just want to make no plans at all—just do whatever comes up. What's more important in creating the perfect day, *what* you do or *with whom* you do it?

CHAPTER 4

Boley Bound

We must accept finite disappointment,
but we must never lose infinite hope.

—DR. MARTIN LUTHER KING, JR.

Charlie's mom and dad, Sister Corrine and Reverend Zeke, can recall a perfect day of a different sort. Their perfect day was June 15, 1900. That's the day they "jumped the broom."

"Jumping the broom" is something a bride and groom do at or after their wedding. It's a traditional African ceremony. Some people say it comes from an old African tribal marriage ritual of putting sticks on the ground to represent the couple's new home. Under this custom, the man and the woman jump over a broom to illustrate sweeping away the single life and the old problems and concerns. Crossing over the broom symbolically brings in the new, signaling that the couple has embarked on a fresh journey together as husband and wife.

Charlie learned of the "jumping the broom" ritual the same way he learns so much else: He asked the right question. Barely a day after his fishing excursion with his dad, he began to reflect on what he'd experienced. He realized that he'd just had the perfect day—well, as perfect as any day could be. He'd spent his time in conversation with his dad, and he'd had the kind of one-on-one attention that all kids love. What could be more fulfilling?

Charlie had been thinking about what other people might consider to be the perfect day. He decided to experiment on his mom, just to get some idea.

"Mom, what was your perfect day like—well, if you've ever had one? You've had one haven't you, Mom?"

Bubbling over with excitement, Charlie's mom began to tell Charlie all about her wedding day. It was as if Charlie had suddenly removed the cap from a shaken or dropped Coca-Cola. Words spewed from his mom's mouth. She focused on one part of the wedding festivities: the broom-jumping ceremony. Charlie listened intently.

"Yes, honey, oh, my, yes. I have had a perfect day!" Charlie's mom gushed. "Baby," she began with a distinct air of exhilaration, "After the wedding, we moved into Fellowship Hall at the church for our reception. The first thing we did was to gather folks for the broom jumping ceremony.

"The guests all joined hands and formed a circle around us as we stood in front of the broom. We were dressed to the nines, Zeke in his black tuxedo and me in my lacey white gown.

"I'd carefully decorated the broom with red, black, and green ribbon the previous night. Zeke and I then talked about how it felt to begin a new life together. We asked the guests to help us stay strong and remain committed to each other. Then, the moment of truth arrived. We joined hands. The guests counted down: "Ten, nine, eight, seven, six, five, four, three, two, one— JUMP!" As the guests whooped and hollered, we leapt over the broom and into our life as a couple."

After getting married—"tying the knot"— Charlie's folks had to find a place to live and raise the family they didn't yet have but both wanted. They chose Oklahoma because they'd heard so much about it. At the time, this place called Oklahoma offered all kinds of opportunity: lots of available land, no overcrowding, and a place so new that it didn't have laws that treated white folks and colored folks differently.

They thought, "What better place to start a new life. Oklahoma, here we come!"

They narrowed their choices down to two locations in Oklahoma: a city called Tulsa and a unique small town named Boley. Reverend Zeke, who'd listened in silence to Sister Corrine's description of their wedding day, eagerly chimed in. He pointed out to Charlie the distinct features of

each of the two possible homes they'd considered. Each place held promise, though they were
as different as night and day.

"Tulsa, Son, is a town on the move. Why,
since it became a city back in 1898, it's mushroomed. Some folks call it 'The Magic City;' others, 'The City with Personality.' You know,
drillers discovered oil some time back—still dis-
covering it, as a matter of fact. That find—un-
earthing that black gold—made many a man
rich, and some men even millionaires. It's not
just the white folks, Son. We've got some well-off
colored folk down Tulsa way, too!

"Son, the colored community in Tulsa—the
'Greenwood District'—is fast becoming a nationally
renowned business center. Why, it's far more
grand today than when your mother and I first
looked at it. Folks say that none other than Dr.
Booker T. Washington dubbed the community
'Negro Wall Street' for its famous bustling business climate. Greenwood attracts the best and
the brightest of our race from all over America.
These folks come to Tulsa seeking new opportunities and fresh challenges. For some, Tulsa is
like the Promised Land."

"Opportunities," Charlie mused. "How is it
opportunity when the colored people in Tulsa
can't live or work where they want; if they're
forced to live in some small section of the city because of segregation?"

"You know how we're separate by law, Son,
and by custom, too. That's just the way it is—at

least for now," Reverend Zeke acknowledged with an air of resignation.

"That may sound bad, having to live apart and go to different schools and all, but there's some good in even the worst of things," he continued. "The separation means that we coloreds have to do business among ourselves. In the case of the Greenwood in Tulsa, that means that many colored folks are doing well by trading with one another, doing business with one another. The dollars stay within the Greenwood community because that's the way it has to be by law. We can't freely shop and spend in most of the white establishments, so we buy from and sell to our own down there in Greenwood. We just don't let those Jim Crow segregation laws get us down.

"Son, I know you've heard it said that money talks. Well, that's true. Don't get me wrong. Money isn't everything. Still, when we colored folk support our own and create wealth, we gain power. Power is what will get us the respect we deserve from the white folks. When they see that we can stand on our own two feet, maybe things will change."

"Okay, Dad, I think I understand," nodded Charlie knowingly. "So, how much power do the colored folks in Tulsa have? Do they help run the city? Are there colored people in Tulsa who are as rich as white people? Do they drive fancy automobiles, live in fine homes, and dress up in expensive clothes?"

"Some power, Son, some power," his dad replied. "They don't run the city, although I've heard they have at least one colored police officer in town—a man called Barney Cleaver. Colored folks in Tulsa have power, but it's all in their own section of town.

"Some of the people in Greenwood have become sophisticated business tycoons. Why, an enterprising man named Mr. Simon Berry developed his transportation businesses around the needs of the community. His nickel-a-ride jitney service using a topless Model-T Ford is the talk of the town. He also runs other businesses. Folks say Mr. Simon Berry makes as much as $500 a day sometimes. Can you believe that—$500 a day? Why, Son, I don't make that much in a month of Sundays!"

"Oh, boy, Dad," Charlie said, "What I would do with that kind of money! I could have my own car, buy a boat, wear fancy, tailor-made suits— even traipse off to Europe! And you said that there are more men like Mr. Berry in Tulsa?"

"Definitely, Son, definitely," Reverend Zeke responded. "And there are a few successful women, too. One of them is Mrs. Mabel B. Little. She runs a beauty salon down in Greenwood.

"Mr. James Lee Northington, Sr. is a successful colored building contractor. He's also a flying man, what folks call an 'aviator.'

"Then there's Dr. A. C. Jackson, called the most able Negro surgeon in America by the Mayo brothers of the famous Mayo Clinic up there in

Minnesota. He treats both colored and white pa-
tients. Now you know that man must be good!

"Oh, and there's A. J. Smitherman. He's the
editor and publisher of the *Tulsa Star*, the colored newspaper."

"Wow, Dad, that's amazing! Tell me more—
there must be more," Charlie roared. "Greenwood in Tulsa sounds like an incredible place!"

"Son, there are also whole families of successful people in Tulsa. Take, for example, the
Williams family. The Williams family owns and
operates several businesses, including the
Williams Dreamland Theatre, a confectionery—
that's a candy store, Son—and a garage. The
Williams' rooming house sits atop the theatre
along Greenwood Avenue.

"Son, Greenwood truly comes alive on
Thursday night. That's 'maid's night off' in Tulsa.
Colored women who work in the homes of rich
white folks take advantage of the day's opportunity to gussie up and stroll down Greenwood
way. I'm telling you, Son, those lovely ladies rival
the elegant models on a Paris runway."

"What about the teachers, Dad?" Charlie
asked. "Do they have good schools with great
teachers in Greenwood? You've always said that
a town is only as good as its people, and that the
people need to be educated."

"I don't want to forget the teachers, Son.
Tulsa has more than its fair share of great ones,
like E. W. Woods. He's been the principal of
Booker T. Washington High School since 1913.

What's really incredible is how he got to Tulsa. He actually arrived in Tulsa by foot from Memphis, Tennessee, in answer to a call for colored teachers. Imagine that—walking from Memphis to Tulsa! That man wanted to work, didn't he? And he's made quite a name for himself if you ask me.

"Mr. Woods expects a great deal from his students. He tells them they're as good as ninety percent of the people and better than the rest. And guess what? They usually prove him right. So you remember that, too, Son. You're as good as ninety percent of the other kids, and you're better than the rest! I expect at least as much from you as Mr. Woods expects from his students. Understand?"

"Yes, sir, I do," Charlie replied, nodding affirmatively as he spoke. "I do understand, and I won't ever let you down, Dad!"

"From movie theatres to lawyers' offices, from grocery stores to schools, from beauty salons to shoeshine shops, Greenwood has it all, Son. In fact, some folks claim that Greenwood even rivals such famous thoroughfares as bluesy Beale Street in Memphis and fancy State Street in Chicago.

"Greenwood is magnificent. But we just weren't ready for life in the big city. We're simple, country folks. We wanted to live someplace just a bit slower and more peaceful. Besides, there's talk now that trouble might be brewing up there in Tulsa.

"The word on the street is that some white folks are a mite jealous of the colored folks' success down in Greenwood. Then, too, the Ku Klux Klan is gaining a foothold in Oklahoma and elsewhere. You know the KKK likes nothing more than stirring up commotion between the colored and white folks. KKK spells nothing but trouble!

"Why, I've heard that some colored folks have even had notes posted on their doors warning them to leave town or face the consequences. That, Son, is enough to frighten anybody!

"So, Tulsa had its pluses and its minuses. Truth be told, we were looking for someplace closer to nature. We wanted wide open space and big blue sky. So, we chose Boley, a little town in this great big country of ours."

By the time Reverend Zeke and Sister Corrine arrived in Boley in 1905, the town had gained a reputation as a growing colored community where anything was possible.

"Son, by the time you grow up," Reverend Zeke once told him, "There won't be a need for separate towns for colored people like ours."

Reverend Zeke figured that by then people would have learned to live together in peace. Time, he thought, would heal old wounds.

The idea for creating the town of Boley started with a bet, a small wager between two men, each of whom had something to prove. Reverend Zeke tells the story as well as anyone could.

"Well, Charlie, it's a long story, but it all

began on a steamy Oklahoma spring afternoon. Two men began debating whether colored people could run their own towns. After all, in the minds of many white people, we colored folks couldn't do anything on our own. We were supposed to be inferior—somehow less than the white folks.

"Well, one of the men thought that colored people were just as good as white people; that they could be successful if they were given a fair chance. The other man bet that colored people didn't have the intelligence and skills to run a town. So, the two men, Mr. Moore and Mr. Boley, decided to conduct a little experiment—they made a wager, really. They purchased land in the Creek Nation, Indian Territory, from an Indian freedman and sold it in lots to colored families. That's how Boley began in 1903."

"I'm sure you know which of the two men was right: The man who bet on Boley's success. Schools, businesses, and churches sprang up," Reverend Zeke said.

"Just look around you today, boy. Everything is owned and operated by colored people. Even the mayor, the sheriff and other city leaders are all colored people.

"We're not the only colored town in Oklahoma, you know. There are others like Tullahassee, Red Bird, Rentiesville, Langston, Clearview, and Taft, just to name a few. Just like Boley, those towns are colored: colored born and bred; colored through and through."

"There's no longer any doubt about what colored people are capable of if we're given a chance," Reverend Zeke concluded. "We can do it all, Son; we can do it all," he declared.

Reverend Zeke wasn't the only one who had faith in the ability of colored people. In fact, in 1904 Dr. Booker T. Washington came to town. Reverend Zeke called Dr. Washington the most famous colored man in the world. He started a college in Alabama called Tuskegee Institute, and he worked for the rights of colored people. Reverend Zeke understood the importance of a ringing endorsement of Boley from a man of Dr. Washington's stature.

"Lord, Son, when news of Dr. Washington's visit hit town, it spread like wildfire. It was the biggest thing that had happened in Boley in its whole history. Everybody who was anybody dropped everything to be there."

"Son, I wish you could have seen it. The whole town took on a relaxed, carefree, joyous mood. People poured into town: young ones, old ones; tall ones, short ones; skinny ones, fat ones. Loud, uniformed marching bands, fancy motor cars, and beautifully groomed horses paraded past the sparkling windows of the downtown businesses. Smiling vendors peddled hot dogs and all manner of popular sweet treats: taffy, peanut brittle, licorice, and more."

"That day, Son, ordinary people looked extraordinary. The women wore colorful, sophisticated outfits; the men donned dark, elegant suits. Wide-brimmed hats crowned many a woman's head. Those without hats sported freshly pressed and curled hair. Most of the men styled in dark-colored fedoras; a few bareheaded souls showed off the latest haircuts.

"The men looked like princes; the women, princesses. They strolled merrily down both sides of busy, noisy Main Street, watching and being watched. You could feel the excitement in the air. The joy dangled like fog on a cool fall morning. The murmur of anticipation carried in the wind."

The people were just part of what made Dr. Washington's visit so memorable. Reverend Zeke continued, "Son, that day seemed like our own little world's fair. And what's a fair without tasty food and snappy music?"

"You know how I like my grub, Son. Well, I made some tough choices that day. The sweet smells of mouth-watering, hickory smoked barbecue and tender, crispy Southern fried chicken alternated between my nostrils. I couldn't decide which smell I liked the most, so I bought some of both. Lord knows I spent a week's wages in a matter of hours, but I had no regrets! And the music—talk about a bargain. It doesn't get any cheaper than free!

"From the North and the South, and from the East and the West," Reverend Zeke said excitedly, "lively music filled the air like helium in a dime-store balloon." He continued, "It was as though the music lifted the clouds higher and higher into the sky. The clouds appeared to float on each note.

"Son, back then, Dr. Washington electrified audiences throughout the country with his powerful speeches. He was truly a sight to behold. Many people liked what he had to say about improving relations between colored people and white people. He became a statesman—kind of like an ambassador for the government.

"Dr. Washington was as proud of Boley as we were of him. He bragged to the huge, star-struck crowd about the success he saw in our town. He even called Boley the most enterprising of the Negro towns that he had visited.

"Dr. Washington said that the people of Boley set a fine example for what colored people in America could accomplish if white folks only gave them a chance. He encouraged the children at the Boley school to do their best, and to work to make Boley the best little town in America."

Charlie had always looked up to Dr. Washington. He admired the things Dr. Washington did for colored people—for the country—during his lifetime. Just as he encouraged kids to do, Charlie always did his best in school. He vowed to make something out of himself; to make his parents proud.

CHAPTER 5

The Mystery of Our History

*Just as a tree without roots is dead,
a people without history or culture
also becomes a dead people.*

—MALCOLM X

Sometimes there are important bits of history that seem to percolate just beneath the surface. Charlie unearthed some fascinating information about his own school and town.

"My school may not be the newest or the nicest school in the world, but it's special to me. It's like my home away from home. One of the things I've learned at school is our school history. One man made a big difference for my school and many others like it.

"Tens of thousands of dollars from a man named Julius Rosenwald helped build many schools for colored children here in Oklahoma and in other parts of the country. His money helped build the Boley school.

"Colored kids and white kids don't go to school together. That's the law. In most places with separate colored schools, the colored facilities are cramped and crumbling in comparison to the white schools.

"Materials and supplies in the colored schools are not as good, either. In fact, our books are often hand-me-downs from the white schools.

"Colored kids in many places have to travel right past nearby white schools to get to faraway colored schools. What kind of sense does that make?

"It's tough, believe me, but living in a place like Boley, where almost everyone's colored, makes things easier. Mr. Rosenwald's support makes a big difference!

"Mr. Rosenwald, president of Sears, Roebuck, & Company and a world-famous businessman, makes lots of money. Have you heard of Sears, Roebuck & Company? It's one of America's top retail department stores. Mr. Rosenwald came up with two ideas that made Sears so successful.

"He originated the 'money-back guarantee.' That just means that if you buy something at Sears and you aren't happy with it, you can take it back and get a refund.

"Mr. Rosenwald's other idea helped Sears become a leader in the mail order business. He developed a system that makes it easier and quicker to get things from Sears by mail.

Because of that, you don't have to go into a Sears store to buy things. You can just order them from the Sears catalogue. Before you know it, your order will arrive in the U.S. Mail.

"With all his money, Mr. Rosenwald become what's known as a philanthropist. I know—it's a big word. It's probably the biggest word I know, but its meaning is simple. A philanthropist is someone like Mr. Rosenwald who uses his money to help others by supporting important parts of the community.

"I know you're wondering, 'Why does a philanthropist give?' Well, in the case of Mr. Rosenwald, maybe it's because he grew up Jewish and poor. He knows how it feels to be different and to do without things that many others take for granted. He understands what it feels like to be part of a group that some people don't like and don't always respect. Because of his own life experiences, Mr. Rosenwald understands colored people and can relate to the struggles they go through.

"Mr. Rosenwald believes deeply in education for all children. He's made it his business to get involved and make a positive difference. He uses his money to try to make it possible for all children, no matter what color, to get the best education possible. Because of all the good things Mr. Rosenwald does, his picture hangs in the hallway of my school."

Of course, there's much more to Boley than just a school. One of the highly-anticipated an-

nual events in town—and one of Boley's best
kept secrets—is its extravagant, world-class carnival.

Scarcely a week had passed since Charlie
and his dad spent a full day together, fishing in
the Dukes' pond. On this day, though, they
spent a partial evening doing what they did
best—talking—in their small but tidy backyard.
Reverend Zeke told Charlie about the 1905 carnival, one of the highlights of that year.

"Back in 1905, folks came from all around to
take part in the carnival and to look at Boley as
a possible future home," Reverend Zeke boasted.
"The Fort Smith & Western Railroad offered half-
price tickets to Boley from Fort Worth and
Houston, Texas.

"That year, many well-known colored speak-
ers came for the carnival. Some of the best colored bands in the area played. Even the world-
famous Fisk Jubilee Singers came to town all the
way from Nashville, Tennessee.

"Son, there's nothing like the Fisk Jubilee
Singers. When those young folks sing those sad,
heart-felt spirituals, even grown men weep. Why,
they've toured all over the world. Imagine that—
a bunch of colored college kids singing their way
around the globe, and being treated almost like
royalty. I never thought I'd see the day!

"By the way, Son, the power in those spirituals that the Fisk Jubilee Singers sing comes from
their roots in slavery. They're really just songs
that bring together the pain, the suffering, and,

yes, the hope that the slaves felt. I think of spirituals as survival songs, Son. They made life bearable for our people when it seemed unbearable."

"Well, Dad," Charlie asked quizzically, "What did they do when they weren't in church? I mean, they didn't sing spirituals at work and at other places, did they?"

"Yes and no," his dad offered paradoxically. "Yes, some people sang spirituals in places other than church. But no, spirituals were by no means the only type of music. Remember when we talked about field hollers and the blues, Son—back on our fishing trip? It's all related."

"Right, Dad, right!" Charlie exclaimed, recalling the interconnectedness of the various types of music colored people—his people—originated. "Now tell me more about the 1905 Boley carnival," he urged.

"Oh, all right—that's enough! You're right. You know if you get me started talking about music I can go on forever. Now let me finish telling you about that unforgettable 1905 Boley carnival," Reverend Zeke interjected.

"There were also afternoon baseball games between the Indian tribes. The rivalry between the Creeks and the Seminoles was especially exciting. To top everything off, the carnival featured mule racing, bronco busting, and a calf-roping contest.

"Son, that year, in 1905, five thousand people came to Boley for the carnival—and everyone behaved. Things went without a hitch, orderly and peaceful all the time. No one left disappointed. Boley was and still is a little colored town with a big heart of gold."

Charlie loves carnivals, but he's a rodeo fan, too. He's especially fond of one rodeo cowboy known 'round the world.

"Today, we have a carnival plus a rodeo in Boley. We have great cowboys here, but none to match my greatest rodeo hero, Bill Pickett. From what Dad told me and from what I've read on my own, I think Bill Pickett is the greatest cowboy ever!

"Thousands of cowboys look up to Mr. Pickett. Why, he's the greatest colored cowboy in the whole world, and one of the best of all the cowboys, colored or white. He's got roots right here in Oklahoma, working over on the 101 Ranch near Ponca City.

"Dad told me that the 101 Ranch is like nothing he's ever seen anywhere else. He said it's amazing!"

"Son," Charlie's dad noted, "That 101 Ranch is something to behold. It sprawls across four counties of leased Indian lands. Not only is it a showplace; it's also a working ranching employing thousands of people. The 101 Ranch has a school, general store, show grounds, café, hotel, newspaper, magazine, blacksmith shop, leather shop, dairy, saddle shop, meat packing plant, and an oil refinery. The 101 Ranch has its own scrip—its own money. There are homes there for employees, guest houses, and even a Dude Ranch. They also breed animals and develop agricultural products there.

"Son," Charlie's dad continued, "The 101 Ranch Wild West Show travels all over the world. It's like a giant rodeo, featuring roping, riding, bulldogging, Indian dancers, trick roping, shooting, and more. Boy, oh boy, that's some kind of entertainment, now isn't it?"

"Yeah, Dad, it certainly is," Charlie said, grinning and nodding approvingly. "That's entertainment for sure!"

Bill Pickett, the son of former slaves, made "bulldogging"—some people call it "steer wrestling"—popular. That's where a cowboy on horseback rides alongside a steer, grabs it by the horns, jumps down from the horse, and wrestles the steer to the ground.

Reverend Zeke met Bill Pickett once. "Son," he said, his voice rising as he became more excited, "That Bill Pickett would climb into the saddle of his appaloosa stallion, then fly out of the chute like a flaming arrow shot from a tightly strung bow. Alongside him there would be a giant steer, snarling and spitting, its red eyes bulging wide as if they were filled with fire. Pickett would catch hold of the steer and lock onto its horns. Then, like a bolt of lightning, he'd jump down on it with all his might. In just seconds, he'd fearlessly tackle the bull, leaving it pinned, helpless, and ready to surrender.

"Bill Pickett, Son, is a real rodeo cowboy, a

true star. He's even been halfway around the world in 'Wild West' shows, displaying his roping, riding, and bulldogging skills in places like Canada, Mexico, South America, and England. No steer ever gave him a serious challenge. Folks say that before long, even the bulls trembled in fear when they heard the name Bill Pickett."

Like Bill Pickett, the town of Boley gained quite a reputation. It became one of the top little towns in the country for colored people because of its schools, businesses, churches, and social activities. That's how Reverend Zeke and Sister Corrine wound up in Boley. That's how Boley became Charlie's hometown.

CHAPTER 6

All in the Family

If you don't know [your family's] history,
then you don't know anything. You are a leaf
that doesn't know it is part of a tree.

—MICHAEL CRICHTON

Charlie's dad often tells him stories about how the Jackson family and other colored families came to Oklahoma. He believes that understanding the past is essential to life in the present and in the future. Reverend Zeke is equal parts storyteller and teacher. He's part what the French call a *raconteur* (a fantastic storyteller) and part what the Hindus call a *swami* (a special teacher). This particular Sunday's dinnertime conversation turned into a lesson about family.

"Certain things should never be forgotten, Son," Reverend Zeke instructed sternly. "They need to be passed on from generation to generation. Our history is one of those things. Since you're our only child, I want to be sure to pass our family history down to you. I'm your personal griot."

An awkward silence ensued. "Ah...okay... So, what's a griot, Dad?" asked Charlie haltingly, clueless as to what this strange-sounding word might mean.

"A 'griot,' Son, is an African storyteller—a person who shares knowledge, wisdom, and, above all else, history, with his people," Reverend Zeke pointed out. "Griots occupy a special place in many African societies because they're considered so important. Some day you'll be the family griot, so listen carefully to what I say."

Many kids get bored when their parents go on and on and on about all their relatives. They fidget, squirm, and scowl when their folks lecture to them about family history that doesn't seem to be important. Charlie's just the opposite. He thinks knowing about the past helps him understand the present and plan for his future. He hopes that if we can only figure out why things happened, then maybe we could learn to keep the bad things from recurring and find ways to make the good things happen all over again. He sees learning about his own family as his most important history lesson.

"I can see so much about my family by just watching Mom and Dad," Charlie reflected. "They're like mirrors. I can see things about myself in both of them. It's not just how I look. Sometimes I do and say the same things that they do and say. They tell me all of the time how they are so much like their own parents. It's funny how we're all tied together. Like the branches of a tree, we're different in some ways, but we've got the same roots."

"Speaking of roots, wouldn't it be wonderful if you could talk to all the people who have ever been in your family? Who knows, you could be the descendant of royalty or something! I mean, think about the things you could ask someone in the family who lived long ago. What kinds of questions would you ask?

"My Dad shares all our family history with me. I don't have to ask many questions. He's told me about his parents and Mom's parents many times. I guess hearing about them from Dad is the next best thing to really being able to talk to them myself. I can hear the story now."

"Charlie, my folks, Solomon and Queen Esther Jackson—proud folks with proud names—were both born slaves in the backwoods of Tennessee," Reverend Zeke explained.

"Slaves. Can you imagine that, Son—your grandparents? Can you imagine being owned by somebody just because of the color of your skin? Can you imagine life without freedom? Can you imagine being treated as something less than human?"

"No, Dad, never," Charlie responded insistently. "I would've run away."

"Son, times were different back then," Charlie's dad noted calmly but firmly. "They didn't know another way of life. Slave owners denied them access to a basic education. Those who got an education did so secretly, and at their own peril. Those who dared to attempt an escape faced certain death if caught."

"Well, I'd rather be dead than to be a slave," a defiant, stone-faced Charlie said in a matter-of-fact tone.

"Well, Son," Reverend Zeke said with a sigh, "I understand what you're saying, but I know that you don't really mean that. Times were different, like I said. Folks did the best they could with what they had. That's what they all did. They did what they had to do just to survive. That's what my folks did. That's how they endured. If they hadn't, I wouldn't be here today. Neither would you, Son. Neither would you.

"By the time I was born in 1880, slavery had ended, and the so-called 'Reconstruction' had collapsed. Reconstruction was supposed to rebuild the South and put the Negroes on equal footing with whites after the Civil War ended. Well, that just didn't happen, Son.

"Oh, some things got rebuilt all right, and a few colored folks got good jobs and government offices. But relations between the white and the colored didn't improve much. The gains we made didn't last long. Once again, colored folk wound up a couple of feet behind instead of on equal footing when all was said and done."

About the time Charlie's dad got really wound up in his family history, his mom, Sister Corrine, interrupted to shift the conversation to her side of the family. That's the side with all the Indian blood.

"My folks, Joe Red Eagle, a mixed-blood Indian tribal chief with Cherokee and Creek heritage, and Sarah Jane Johnson, a Creek freedman, grew up in Oklahoma, baby," Charlie's mom proudly noted. A Creek Indian freedman is a colored person who had been owned as a slave by the Creek Indians, but later gained freedom. They settled up near Tulsa. In fact 'Tulsa' is a form of an Indian word that means 'old town.'

"Anyway, like I said, Daddy was a chief; Mama was a freedman. "Grandpa Joe and Grandma Sarah lived in what was called 'Indian Territory,' Son. Separate Indian nations like the Creek Nation, the Choctaw Nation, and the Cherokee Nation made up Indian Territory. They used to tell me stories about how the federal government forced their ancestors to come to Oklahoma from down around Georgia."

"Forced, Mom? What do you mean by 'forced'? How can you force a whole group of people out of one place and into another?" Charlie queried.

"Well, baby," Charlie's mom replied, "It helps when you've got thousands of soldiers there to enforce the order to move. They called it the 'Trail of Tears'—*Nunna daul Tsuny*, meaning 'the trail where they cried,' in Cherokee. My, oh my! Lord knows my people shed many a tear back in those dark days.

"The government removed Indian folk from

their lands in the South and marched them up here to Oklahoma. They say the Indians agreed by treaty to the removal, but our people were tricked and betrayed. They say it was all legal, but it simply wasn't right."

Charlie's mom continued, "So, in the 1830s and 1840s Indians gave up their homelands and settled here in Oklahoma. Just imagine thousands of men, women, children being removed from their homelands, herded into forts, and then forced to march a thousand miles in the midst of a brutal winter. Some made the journey by boat under equally bleak conditions. So many folks took sick and died on the way—thousands! Son, so many lives were lost so needlessly in what can only be called a death march. Our people lost our land, lost friends and relatives, and lost part of our way of life.

"We're strong, though, Son. Our people are strong. Enough of us endured so that we survived, and we're still here today. I wouldn't be here today if it weren't for that strength," Sister Corrine noted, eyes moist with the pain of memory. "Always remember. Never forget.

"The other part of what is now Oklahoma, called 'Oklahoma Territory,' remained unsettled until the Oklahoma Land Run of 1889 opened it up for settlement by non-Indians. By then, everybody wanted a piece of the action.

"In 1907, the Twin Territories—Indian Territory and Oklahoma Territory—joined together to create the state of Oklahoma.

Oklahoma became the forty-sixth state of the Union. By the way, did you know that the word 'Oklahoma' comes from the Choctaw Indian language and means 'land of the red people'? Remember that, Son. This land is named for us. You should be proud of that part of you that's Indian, Son. It's a mighty fine combination, black and red; mighty fine, indeed!"

Many colored people escaped from the South to Oklahoma seeking a brighter future. Good jobs were hard to find for colored people in the South. Besides that, tough conditions in the South made life miserable. Some people did everything they could to keep colored people from being successful. Threats and actual violence were commonplace.

Blood-thirsty mobs murdered colored people for crimes they did not commit. Sometimes colored people paid with their lives for violating so-called "Jim Crow" laws.

Jim Crow laws make it illegal for colored people and white people to ride the same trains, sit in the same waiting areas, use the same restrooms, and drink from the same water fountains. There are even laws that make it almost impossible for colored people to vote.

They shot them. They stabbed them. They burned them. They dismembered them. They hanged them. These mobs—groups of men who took the law into their own hands—terrorized entire communities, and put fear in the hearts of innocent colored people.

That sort of mob intimidation and violence targeting colored people is called lynching. It almost happened to Charlie's dad. The story Reverend Zeke told Charlie's about his ordeal in the South is typical.

"Son," Charlie's dad sighed, "I just barely made it out of Tennessee alive. The night before I left Memphis, a mob came for me. I knew what that meant. Why, back in 1892 a Memphis mob lynched three colored men—successful businessmen—out of pure jealousy and spite. It so angered Ms. Ida B. Wells that she wrote newspaper articles about the horrors of lynching and went on an anti-lynching crusade.

"Well, my situation started with a rumor— the kind of rumor that could get you killed down South; still can, in fact. Someone spread a tale that I'd whistled at a some rich white lady, the wife of a well-known Memphis banker. Of course it wasn't true, but that didn't matter. Mobs don't care about the truth unless, of course, it's *their* truth.

"Lucky for me, I knew that the mob was coming, so I hid in a neighbor's closet, shaking, sweating, and doing my best to keep quiet. When the coast was clear, I sneaked out of town with only the clothes on my back, leaving everything I'd worked so hard for behind. If it hadn't been for my neighbor, Herschel Washington, I wouldn't be here today. He risked his own life by saving mine."

Many people felt that they'd come to a fork in

the road. They could either stay in the South, mistreated in every way, or start afresh in Oklahoma. They wanted to own their own land. They wanted to live in peace. They wanted to make a decent living for themselves and their families. Was that really too much to ask?

Reverend Zeke came to Oklahoma in 1895. Sister Corrine was already there.

"I made my way to Oklahoma for a clean start," Reverend Zeke explained. "I'd heard that Oklahoma offered opportunity—lots of land that anyone could own, safety from mob violence, and a chance to earn a decent living.

"For a time that was mostly true. Some colored folks made quite a name for themselves here in Oklahoma before statehood. One of them was Edward P. McCabe. I'll tell you more about him a bit later. After statehood, Oklahoma started to mimic the South when it came to relations between the races. When Oklahoma became a state in 1907, the first laws passed established segregation in the state.

"Before official segregation took hold in Oklahoma—before statehood, that is—that fellow I mentioned, E. P. McCabe, was like a colored celebrity here. I'd heard of him when I was back in Tennessee. Folks spoke of this smart, popular, colored businessman and politician who was encouraging colored people to come to Oklahoma. McCabe came to Oklahoma from Kansas."

"Mr. McCabe served as the Kansas State Auditor for four years. An auditor is someone

who keeps track of all the money. He was the
highest colored official in the Kansas government.

"McCabe moved to Oklahoma in 1889. He
took part in the great Oklahoma Land Run. On
April 22, 1889, at precisely noon, a trumpet
sounded. The blaring trumpet signaled the thousands of folks who'd gathered on foot and on
horseback all along the Oklahoma border that
Oklahoma Territory was open for settlement. It
became the largest one-day settlement of land in
American history. McCabe knew what an opportunity this was, so he came down from Kansas to
take part in the festivities.

"You know about the Land Run, right, Son?
It was free land, so folks came from as far as
Europe to claim plots of 160 acres. Some folks
jumped the gun, going in before noon that day.
They staked their claims, and then hid from pa-
trolling soldiers. Folks called them 'Sooners,'
since they went in sooner than they were supposed to. Most of those Sooners got their land:
first come, first served.

"McCabe acquired some land, then began to
use his power and connections to push for the
creation of a colored state right here in
Oklahoma. He even met with the twenty-third
president of the United States, Benjamin
Harrison.

"National leaders, even Congressmen and
Senators, encouraged the creation of a colored
state. They introduced a bill in Congress,"

Reverend Zeke emphasized. "Certain groups of people came together to resist his efforts. Even the famous *New York Times* mocked the idea. McCabe's dream of an all-colored state faded.

"McCabe came up with a new plan. He founded a townsite company. He started to establish separate towns for colored people in Oklahoma. He founded the town of Langston.

"Son, Mr. McCabe helped start it all. He's one of the reasons that our family ended up in Oklahoma."

Thanks to the work of "boosters" like Mr. McCabe, colored towns began to pop up all over Oklahoma. Boosters were people who encouraged disillusioned colored folks, primarily from the South, to come to Oklahoma. They made Oklahoma sound like a milk-and-honey paradise, a place of beauty and bounty.

Mr. McCabe wrote bulletins that talked about freedom and opportunity in Oklahoma. He hired agents to go into the South and talk to unhappy colored people about the chance to make a new start in the colored towns.

McCabe and other boosters often exaggerated. They engaged in "puffery"—making too-good-to-be-true statements about their product—Oklahoma—in order to entice people to move to the state. However, the boosters did offer adventure and new possibilities for folks whose faith had been tested and whose hopes had been dashed.

Charlie understands and identifies with the

movement to establish colored towns like his own, Boley. He has a particular fondness for Langston, the colored town McCabe established in 1890.

"Dad wants me to go to the college for colored students in Langston," said Charlie. It's called 'Colored Agricultural and Normal University,' but most people just call it 'Langston' for short. I'll be the first person in my family to go to college.

"I already know what I want to study when I go to Langston. I want to study government and history. Then, I want to go somewhere to law school—who knows, maybe even to Harvard! Imagine that—a colored boy from Boley, Oklahoma at Harvard. I'm going to be the first member of my family to go to college. You can count on that! Conceive. Believe. Achieve.

"I figure that when I become a lawyer I will work against some of the laws that exist in Oklahoma—especially the Jim Crow laws. This is wrong—dead wrong! I want to change it.

"Colored people in the South felt that they had no opportunity to make a decent life there, so many of them fled. They, along with colored freedmen who were already in Oklahoma, created colored towns like Boley. They made it possible for me to succeed.

"They gave me a great gift—a wonderful place to grow up. In my little town, I can be who I really am deep down inside. I feel welcome and warm and safe. Nobody tells me that I'm not good enough or smart enough.

"Dad said that we are blessed to live in a town where we are free to do and be what we want to do and be. Here, a boy like me really can be anything he wants to be.

"'Son,' he says, 'you've got everything you need to be successful: a sound mind, a good heart, and a strong will. Those things will make you a winner.'

"Dad missed just one thing: I've got two wonderful parents who love me. There's no place like home."

Conclusion

If you could choose any place in the whole wide world to live, where would it be? Would you pick a big, bustling American city like New York or Chicago? How about one of the famous European capitals like London, England or Paris, France? What about someplace foreign and exotic, someplace off the beaten path—maybe Sao Paolo, Brazil, Bombay, India, or even Addis Ababa, Ethiopia? And *how* would you choose? What things would you consider? Which of those things would most influence your decision?

Charlie faced these questions on a school assignment—Mrs. Taylor's first semester Language Arts essay. Upon reflection, he wrote an uncharacteristically decisive response.

"I'm not always great at decision-making, but I know how I'd decide these questions," he began. "I've actually thought about this already. In my geography and history classes, I've read about many fascinating cities here in America and around the world. I've studied about Boston and Berlin; San Francisco and Shanghai; Montreal and Madrid, just to name a few. But studying a place isn't the same as being there. Just imagine actually traveling to all those places that you can only dream about now. Wouldn't it be exciting to see how the rest of the world lives; to see if it really is a small world after all?

"I think that it would be great fun to visit all the places that most of us will only hear about. Remember, I said *visit.* There's a big difference between visiting a place for a week or two and living in it day after day after day. I'm just not so sure that I'd want to stay long in any of my fantasy locations. Just thinking about being away from home for a long time scares me. Although I'm slightly embarrassed to admit it, I think I'd be homesick after the first day. Maybe I'm a bit of a 'mama's boy,' but home is where I belong.

"Sometimes I wonder how life would feel if people didn't care about and believe in me. But before I start to worry too much about it, I just count my blessings. I know how lucky I am. I hope that you have people who care about you and believe in you.

"Dad once asked me, 'Charlie, what do you think makes a good town a great town? What makes someplace feel like home?' After thinking about it for a while, I said, uncertainly, 'I think it's the people.' Dad paused, nodded, and smiled.

'Son,' he said, 'I think our little talks have paid off after all.'

"If I had to choose one place in the world to *live*, not just *visit*, I would select my hometown. For me, it would be an easy decision. Nothing really compares with what I've got now, even though I don't have much: no extra money to spend; no fancy food to eat; no special clothes to wear. But what I do have is even better than money and all the things it can buy. I've got my family, my friends, and a wonderful community. Take it from me: There's no place like home."

Bibliography

Hannibal B. Johnson, *Acres of Aspiration—The All-Black Towns in Oklahoma*. Austin, TX: Eakin Press, 2002.

Hannibal B. Johnson, *Black Wall Street—From Riot to Renaissance in Tulsa's Historic Greenwood District*. Austin, TX: Eakin Press, 1998.

Hannibal B. Johnson, *Up From The Ashes—A Story About Community*. Austin, TX: Eakin Press, 2000.

Robert A. Wilson and Stanley Marcus, eds. *American Greats*. New York: PublicAffairs™ , 1999.

Tom Cowan, Ph.D. and Jack Maguire eds. *Timelines of African-American History—500 Years of Black Achievement*. New York: Roundtable Press, Inc., 1994.

Web Sites

http://www.thebluehighway.com/history.html

http://united-states.asinah.net/american-encyclopedia/wikipedia/1/19/1920.html

http://www.fact-index.com/h/ho/hobo.html

http://www.jcs-group.com/oldwest/wildwestshow/101.html

http://home.earthlink.net/~gfeldmeth/lec.1920s.html

http://northbysouth.kenyon.edu/2002/Music/Pages/spirituals.htm

http://northbysouth.kenyon.edu/2002/Music/Pages/
worksongs.htm
http://northbysouth.kenyon.edu/2002/Music/Pages/
fieldhollers.htm
http://en.wikipedia.org/wiki/Trail_of_Tears
http://www.lkwdpl.org/wihohio/barn-ida.htmfile://
C:\DOCUME~1\user\LOCALS~1\Temp\N2XKG6HS.
htm

Appendix A
Boley, Oklahoma Today

This book is based on historical facts and events. For further information on the all-black towns in Oklahoma, consult *Acres of Aspiration: The All-Black Towns in Oklahoma* by Hannibal B. Johnson.

Boley, founded in 1903 and incorporated in 1905, is one of the more than fifty all-black towns that dotted the Oklahoma landscape from pre-statehood days until the present.

African-Americans of Indian ancestry who received grants of land called allotments from the federal government established some of the all-black towns. Other towns grew with the desire of Southern African-Americans in the late 1800s and early 1900s to live life free of the racism, prejudice, and discrimination they faced. These pioneers helped establish the all-black towns in

Oklahoma, hoping to secure better lives for themselves and their offspring.

Those who had Native American ancestry became known as "Natives." Those who migrated from the South were called "Watchina" or "State Negroes." At times, tension and animosity developed between the groups.

E. P. McCabe, once the highest elected official in the state of Kansas, came to Oklahoma during the 1889 land run. McCabe, who dreamed of carving out an all-black state within Oklahoma Territory, became Oklahoma's foremost black booster. He used written bulletins and personal recruiters to encourage disillusioned blacks in the South to move west.

The efforts of McCabe and others lured thousands to Oklahoma, resulting in a proliferation of all-black towns. The all-black town of Boley grew into one of the more popular, well-known, and prosperous all-black towns in America. Boley included a mix of those with distinct Native American heritage and those with deep Southern roots.

Even the famous African-American statesman and educator, Dr. Booker T. Washington, visited Boley. On his visit, he congratulated those who created the town and praised who chose to live there. Boley had it all: schools, churches, and stores. The town even boasted several firsts: the nation's first black-owned bank, black-owned electric company, and black-owned telephone company.

Boley's population has dwindled from a peak of some 5,000 to about 550, not including the 500 or so souls locked up in the John Lilley Correctional Center there. Though many of the town's businesses no longer exist, Boley survives. In addition to the state prison facility, an internationally known manufacturer of meat smokers called Smokaroma remains in Boley. A few other small businesses dot the landscape and provide a few jobs. Each year, Boley hosts an all-black rodeo that attracts thousands of visitors, representing all fifty states and even some foreign countries.

Residents recall fondly the golden years—a time when Boley spelled black pride, potential, and progress in America. To them, there's no place like home.

Appendix B

Fast Facts: Oklahoma's All-black Towns

The All-black Towns in Oklahoma
by Hannibal B. Johnson

Prominently in Kansas, then principally in Oklahoma, all-black towns founded by black seekers mushroomed in the post-Reconstruction era. Weary Southern migrants formed their own frontier communities, largely self-sustaining. Black towns offered hope—hope of full citizenship; hope of self-governance; and hope of full participation, through land ownership, in the American dream.

Despite an auspicious beginning, the all-black town movement crested between 1890 and 1910, a time when American capitalism transitioned from agrarian to urban. This and a host of other social and economic factors ultimately sealed the fates of these unique, historic oases. Many perished. Most faded. Only the strong survived. The few that remain serve as testaments to the human spirit and monuments to the power of hope, faith, and community.

The Push for All-black Towns

- Black presence in Oklahoma dates back at least as far as the sixteenth century, when blacks accompanied Spanish explorers to the area.
- Oklahoma was once considered as the site of an all-black state. Senator Henry W. Blair of New Hampshire introduced a bill in favor of the proposal.
- In 1879, blacks migrated in large numbers from the South to the state of Kansas and other parts of the Midwest.
- Many blacks prospered in Oklahoma as members of the various Native American tribes.
- Black freedmen in Oklahoma were known as "Natives," while black immigrants from other areas, particularly the South, were called "Watchina" or "State Negroes."
- Hannibal C. Carter helped establish the Freedmen's Oklahoma Immigration Association in Chicago in 1881.
- Some of the "Sooners" who came to Oklahoma in the great land run of 1889 were black.

- Historically, Oklahoma boasts more all-black towns than any other state.

Edwin P. McCabe
Father of the All-black Town Movement

- McCabe was for a time the highest-ranking black elected state official in Kansas, serving two terms as state auditor (1882 –1886).
- McCabe was a prominent, popular member of the Republican Party in both Kansas and Oklahoma.
- McCabe lived for a time in Nicodemus, Kansas, one of the early and prominent all-black towns.
- Two black ministers, William Smith and Thomas Harris, conceived the idea of creating an all-black town in Nicodemus, Kansas.
- McCabe came to Oklahoma in 1889 at the time of the great land run.
- McCabe founded Langston, Oklahoma, and the *Langston City Herald* newspaper, a propaganda vehicle to encourage migration to the town.
- In 1890, McCabe visited with President Benjamin Harrison intent on convincing him of the wisdom of creating an all-black state in Oklahoma.
- When Oklahoma became a state in 1907, the first official legislative act was the passage of

rigid "Jim Crow" laws. McCabe filed a lawsuit against such measures.

- McCabe died a pauper in Chicago on February 23, 1920.
- McCabe is buried in Topeka, Kansas.

All-black Towns in Oklahoma

- Booker T. Washington visited Boley, Oklahoma, an all-black town, in 1904.
- Booker T. Washington called Boley, Oklahoma, "[t]he most enterprising, and in many ways the most interesting of the Negro towns in the U.S."
- Members of the gang of Charles Arthur "Pretty Boy" Floyd were killed after robbing the Boley bank and killing its president in 1932.
- Boley was the setting for a movie (*circa* 1920) produced by the Norman Film Manufacturing Company that featured and "all colored" cast. Entitled *The Crimson Skull*, the film co-starred Anita Bush and Lawrence Chenault. Promotional materials described the film as a "baffling western mystery photo-play" featuring "Big Fights, Fast Action...[And] Thrilling Love Scenes."
- Taft, Oklahoma, originally called "Twine, Indian Territory," changed its name in 1908 in honor of President William H. Taft.
- Clearview, Oklahoma, was the site of a vibrant

"Back to Africa" movement led by an African known as "Chief Sam" in 1913.

- Langston, Oklahoma, is the site of the farthest west of all the black colleges.
- Rentiesville, Oklahoma, is the original home of historian Dr. John Hope Franklin.
- Rentiesville, Oklahoma, is the home of guitarist, singer, and noted bluesman D. C. Minner.
- Rentiesville, Oklahoma, is the site of a pivotal Civil War conflict, "The Battle of Honey Springs," also referred to as the "Gettysburg of the West."
- The 1st Kansas Colored Volunteer Infantry Regiment played a key role in the victory of the Federals over the Confederate troops in the Battle of Honey Springs.
- Lelia Foley-Davis, elected mayor of Taft in 1973, became the first elected African-American female mayor in America.
- Red Bird, Oklahoma, reportedly got its name from the fascination of its founder, E. L. Barber, with the number of red birds in the area.

Tulsa's Greenwood District— An All-black Town Within a Town

- O. W. Gurley established the first business, a grocery store, in the Greenwood District in 1905.

- The Williams Theatre in the Greenwood District featured a movie theatre and live entertainment.
- The Greenwood District became known as "Black Wall Street."
- The Greenwood District was the site of the worst race riot in American history, the 1921 Tulsa Race Riot.
- Attorney B. C. Franklin, father of historian Dr. John Hope Franklin, represented some of the victims of the 1921 Tulsa Race Riot.
- The 1921 Tulsa Race Riot Commission was authorized by the Oklahoma Legislature in 1997 to investigate the facts surrounding the Riot and make recommendations on such issues as reparations.
- The 1921 Tulsa Race Riot Commission issued its final report on February 28, 2001.
- The Greenwood District peaked in 1942, boasting some 242 black-owned, black-operated businesses.
- The Greenwood Cultural Center, a multi-million-dollar complex, preserves the vibrant history and culture of the community through art, education, and cultural enrichment.

The Future of the All-black Towns

- Cultural tourism is on the rise. The remaining all-black towns are becoming tourist destinations.

- Both Muskogee Convention & Tourism and Rudisill North Regional Library in Tulsa conduct all-black town tours periodically.
- The Oklahoma Historical Society sponsored the All-Black Town Exhibit, a salute to the all-black towns.
- The All-Black Town Exhibit was housed for a time in the Five Civilized Tribes Museum in Muskogee.
- The Oklahoma Historical Society History Center and Museum features an African-American Gallery that tells the story of the all-black towns.
- One of the keys to the future success of the remaining all-black towns will be the retention of youth and young adults.

Appendix C
Discussion Guide

Following are possible discussion questions, organized by chapter, designed to stimulate thought about the relevance of the book to today's world. The questions are offered as a jumping-off point only. They may prompt equally worthy related (and perhaps unrelated) questions.

Chapter 1: A Place Called Home

1. What differences are there between small towns and big cities? What are the similarities?
2. What does the word "home" mean to you?
3. Do you have a single home or more than one home?
4. List 3 -5 things that make a place "home."

5. How do you define the word "community"?

6. What might be some of the rules a successful community might adopt?

7. Is it possible to belong to more than one community? Explain.

Chapter 2: One More Thing

1. Re-read the poem called "The Iceberg." Does it apply to what you have experienced?

2. Do you think a person's color matters in today's world? Explain.

3. Have you ever had a negative experience based on your race or your color? If so, explain.

4. Besides race and color, what kinds of differences might cause people to treat others less favorably or differently?

5. What does "culture" mean to you?

6. How prevalent is segregation in your hometown?

7. What would be the advantages and disadvantages of living in a place where everyone had the same racial/ethnic identity?

8. What cultures are important parts of your background?

9. Has a personal friend of yours ever had a negative experience based on color? If so, explain.

10. Do you have friends who are different

from you in some way? If so, describe the differences.

11. What are some reasons that differences in people can benefit everyone?

12. What can you do to help make sure that all people are treated fairly?

Chapter 3: The Perfect Day

1. List 3 -5 things that go into making a perfect day.

2. Have you ever had a perfect day? If so, describe it.

3. Is it possible to have a perfect day alone, or must there be someone else with whom to experience it?

4. What impact do gospel, field hollers, and the blues have on music today?

5. Discuss the role of music in your life.

6. Try creating a field holler.

7. What role does your own attitude play in creating the perfect day?

8. Describe what you enjoy doing more than anything else.

Chapter 4: Boley Bound

1. Is there really "no place like home"?

2. What are the best things about your hometown?

3. What would you like to change about your hometown?

4. How would you rate your hometown in comparison to other places you've been?

5. Where do you think you will live when you're finally out of school?

6. What can you do to make the place you live better?

Chapter 5: The Mystery of Our History

1. Why is history important?

2. What things in history interest you most?

3. What things and people make history? Why?

4. What aspects of history would you like to know more about?

5. How are people like you represented in your history books?

6. How do you plan to impact history?

Chapter 6: All in the Family

1. Have you ever attended a family reunion? If so, where and when was it? How did it feel?

2. Have you ever seen your family tree diagramed? If so, describe it.

3. Try sketching your family tree.

4. How much do you know about your family history? Explain.

5. What have your parents, grandparents, or other relatives told you about your family history? Explain.

6. Find a photo of one of your ancestors—someone older than your parents—going back as far as you can. Ask your parents and other relatives about that person. Find out as much as you can. Share the photo and as much of the history of the person depicted in it with a friend and/or with your class.

7. What family traditions would you like to carry on (or start) when you get older?

Appendix D
Words for the Wise—A Glossary

Build your vocabulary with some of the words used in *No Place Like Home.*

A cappella: Without instrumental accompaniment; said of choral singing.

Abolitionist: A person who favors the abolition of some law or custom, especially slavery in the United States.

Barnstorming: Going about the country performing plays, giving lectures, delivering campaign speeches, playing exhibition games, etc., especially in small and rural communities.

Black Sox Scandal: A scandal involving the 1919 baseball World Series in which players on the Chicago White Sox took bribes to throw the series to the Cincinnati Reds.

Blues: A unique musical form involving the merger of African and European traditions;

often associated with lyrics indicating some degree of melancholy.

Booster: A person who promotes something or some cause. African-Americans in Oklahoma (*e.g.*, E.P. McCabe) promoted the Oklahoma as a "Promised Land." They sent written material and agents down to the South to encourage African-Americans to move to Oklahoma.

Bulldogging: Also known as "steer wrestling," this rodeo sport was created by the legendary African-American cowboy, Bill Pickett. In bull-dogging, a cowboy on horseback rides along-side a steer, grabs it by the horns, jumps down from the horse, and wrestles the steer to the ground. The event is timed.

Civil War: The war between the North (the Union) and the South (the Confederacy) in the United States from 1861 to 1865.

Cul-de-sac: A passage (*e.g.*, a street) or position with only one outlet; blind alley.

Culture: The ideas, customs, skills, and arts of a given people in a given period; civilization.

Curfew: A specified time to be a home in the evening or at night.

Field Hollers: Group work songs sung by slaves working in the cotton and rice fields of America; designed to numb the mental pain of slavery and create an environment of coopera-tive work.

Freedman: A person of African descent who had previously been held as a slave. Some freedmen were previously enslaved by the Native American tribes.

Gospel: Spiritual music; with respect to African-Americans, such music often emanates from the legacy of slavery, and expresses the pain, longing, hopes, and aspirations of a people in bondage.

Griot: A storyteller and oral historian in some African traditions.

Hobo: A homeless, itinerant (migratory) worker; hobos were associated with the railroads in the late nineteenth and early twentieth centuries, as they had a reputation for hitching free rides in the baggage cars of trains.

Indian Territory: That part of what is now Eastern Oklahoma which, prior to Oklahoma statehood, was set aside as a territory for the settlement of Native Americans from the Southeastern States who were forced off their tribal lands pursuant to the Indian Removal Acts. Indian Territory existed from 1834 – 1890.

Industrialization: The process of social and economic organization characterized by, among other things, large industries, machine production, and concentration of workers in cities.

Jim Crow: A reference to laws and customs that segregated African-Americans and whites; based on a popular, early nineteenth century minstrel show in which the white performer donned "blackface" makeup.

Jumping the Broom: An African wedding tradition in which the bride and groom jump over a broom to symbolize leaving behind the past and beginning a new life together.

Ku Klux Klan: A secret society of white men founded after the Civil War to reestablish and maintain white supremacy through, among other measures, domestic terrorism aimed primarily at African-Americans.

Lionel train: Operational toy trains sets produced by the Lionel Manufacturing Company; particularly popular during the first half of the twentieth century.

Lynching: A form of vicious intimidation and grotesque violence perpetrated by mob vigilantes directed primarily toward African-Americans generally from the late 1800s through the mid-1900s. Victims of lynching, typically accused of some violation of law or custom, met brutal, ritualistic death, often by hanging, but sometimes by shooting, stabbing, burning, or some combination thereof. Lynching became spectator sport: Crowds often gathered to bear witness.

Oklahoma Land Run: The 1889 opening to general settlement of the Oklahoma Territory in the western part of what became the State of Oklahoma in 1907.

Oklahoma Territory: That part of what is now the State of Oklahoma not included in Indian Territory. Oklahoma Territory officially opened for settlement in 1889.

Philanthropist: A person, often wealthy, who

seeks to help humankind by making gifts to charitable or humanitarian institutions or otherwise funding community/charitable causes or initiatives; a benevolent person.

Prohibition: The forbidding by law of the manufacture, transportation, and sale of alcoholic liquors for beverage purposes. Prohibition extended from 1920 to 1933.

Raconteur: A storyteller.

Reconstruction: The process, after the Civil War, of reorganizing the Southern States which had seceded (*i.e.*, left the Union) and reestablishing them in the Union. Reconstruction lasted from 1867 to 1877.

Segregation: The separation of the races, often by law in the early history of the United States.

Shotgun House: A long, thin, wooden house shaped like a giant rectangle; referred to as a "shotgun house" because one could shoot a shotgun right through the front door of the house and the bullet would travel in a straight line all the way through to the back door.

Slavery: The practice of relegating some human beings to the status of property, subject to the outright ownership and absolute will of another person, often called a "master."

Statesman: A person who exhibits wisdom, skill, and vision in conducting state affairs and addressing public issues; often, someone engaged in the business of government.

Suffrage: The right to vote, especially in political elections; franchise.

Swami: A Hindu title of respect, especially for a religious teacher; a learned person.

Trail of Tears: The designation given the forced migration of the so-called "Five Civilized Tribes" (the Cherokee, Choctaw, Chickasaw, Seminole, and Creek Indians). The Indian Removal Act of 1930, signed into law by President Andrew Jackson, forced these tribes to move from their ancestral homelands in the Southeastern United States to Indian Territory in what is now the State of Oklahoma. "Trail of Tears" is a direct reference to the pain of the uprooting, the brutality of the move itself, and the indifference of the federal government to this tragic human suffering.

Twin Territories: Prior to Oklahoma statehood in 1907, two territories existed there—"Indian Territory" in the east, home to Native American tribes removed from the Southeastern United States; "Oklahoma Territory" in the west, opened to general settlement in the "Land Run" of 1889.

Union: The northern states aligned with the federal government during the American Civil War.

Wells, Ida B. (Barnett) (1862–1931): Ida B. Wells was born in Holly Springs, Mississippi, just months prior to the signing of the Emancipation Proclamation. She graduated from Rust College and became a teacher and newspaper owner/editor in Memphis, Tennessee. She began her crusade against lynching after three African-American Memphis businessmen were lynched in 1892. She married a prominent Chicago attorney, Ferdinand Barnett, in 1895. From Chicago, Ida B. Wells (Barnett) continued to be involved in civil rights issues. The couple had four children.

About the Author

Hannibal B. Johnson, a Harvard Law School graduate, is an author, attorney, and independent consultant specializing in diversity issues and nonprofit governance. He has taught at The University of Tulsa College of Law (legal ethics; legal  writing), Oklahoma State University (leadership and group dynamics; business law), and The University of Oklahoma (ethics; cultural diversity; and race in America). His books, *Black Wall Street—From Riot to Renaissance in Tulsa's Historic Greenwood District, Up From The Ashes—A Story About Community,* and *Acres of*

Aspiration—The All-Black Towns in Oklahoma, chronicle the African-American experience in Oklahoma and its indelible impact on American history. Johnson's *Mama Used To Say—Wit & Wisdom From the Heart and Soul,* is a motivational/inspirational work that centers on the universality of a mother's guidance, nurturance, and love.

CPSIA information can be obtained
at www.ICGtesting.com
Printed in the USA
LVHW081135230721
693314LV00021B/1562

9 781681 791388